FUNNY TRAIL TALES

Outdoor Humor for All Ages

Second Edition

Edited by Amy Kelley Hoitsma

FALCONGUIDES

GUILFORD, CONNECTICUT
HELENA, MONTANA
AN IMPRINT OF ROWMAN & LITTLEFIELD

FALCONGUIDES

© 2000, 2012 Rowman & Littlefield
Previously published by Falcon Publishing, Inc.

FalconGuides is an imprint of Rowman & Littlefield.

Falcon, FalconGuides, and Outfit Your Mind are registered
trademarks of Rowman & Littlefield.

Grateful acknowledgment is made to those who granted permission to reprint the selections in this book. A complete list
of copyright permissions is on page 120.

Library of Congress Cataloging-in-Publication Data is avail-
able on file.

ISBN 978-0-7627-7801-0

Printed in the United States of America

Distributed by NATIONAL BOOK NETWORK

CONTENTS

INTRODUCTION

If I were to give advice on how to stay happy and healthy, two things would surely top my list: Get outside, and laugh—as often as possible. Especially laugh.

If this book is meeting its goals, you've stuffed it in your backpack or thrown it in the trunk of the car, you're on some sort of an outdoor adventure, and now you're ready to relax and read something to make you laugh.

Of course, everyone has his or her own opinion about what's funny, and so I've included something to tickle everyone's funny bone—a wide range of stories that I hope you'll read aloud. Laughing is even better medicine when shared with friends or family.

If you happen to have read the first edition of *Funny Trail Tales*, you might remember a few of my favorites from that book, including Dave Barry's advice on camping, Kathleen Meyer's detailed explanation of how to "go about your business" in the woods, and Howard Tomb's "fine points of expedition behavior" (my favorite being "Do not be cheerful before breakfast").

This edition has eight new pieces by talented and very funny writers, including David Sedaris, Tim Cahill, Garrison Keillor, and Ian Frazier. I've perhaps taken some liberties when it comes to defining the subject of "the outdoors" in this collection (David Sedaris's mother locking him and his siblings out of the house in the middle of winter?), but it's only because these pieces made me laugh out loud.

I hope you have the same response, and that you enjoy this book while enjoying the great outdoors!

Amy Kelley Hoitsma
August 2011

From "Camping" in
*Dave Barry's Only Travel Guide
You'll Ever Need*

DAVE BARRY

Camping: Nature's Way of Promoting the Motel Business

So far we've discussed many exciting travel destinations, but all of them lack an element that is too often missing from the stressful, high-pressure urban environment most of us live in. That element is: dirt. Also missing from the urban environment are snakes, pit toilets, and tiny black flies that crawl up your nose. To experience these things, you need to locate some Nature and go camping in it.

Where Nature Is Located

Nature is located mainly in national parks, which are vast tracts of wilderness that have been set aside by the United States government so citizens will always have someplace to go where they can be attacked by bears. And we're not talking about ordinary civilian bears, either: We're talking about federal bears, which can behave however they want to because they are protected by the same union as postal clerks.

You also want to be on the lookout for federal moose. I had a moose encounter once, when my wife and I were camping in Yellowstone National Park, which is popular with nature lovers because it has dangerous geysers of superheated steam that come shooting up out of the ground, exactly like in New York City, except that the Yellowstone geysers operate on a schedule. Anyway, one morning I woke up and went outside to savor the dawn's ever-changing subtle beauty, by which I mean take a leak, and there, maybe fifteen feet away, was an animal approximately the size of the Western Hemisphere and shaped like a horse with a severe steroid problem. It pretended to be peacefully eating moss, but this was clearly a clever ruse designed to lull me into believing that it was a gentle, moss-eating creature. Obviously no creature gets to be that large by eating moss. A creature gets to be that large by stomping other creatures to death with its giant hooves. Clearly what it wanted me to do was approach it, so it could convert me into a wilderness pizza while bellowing triumphant moss-breath bellows into the morning air. Fortunately I am an experienced woodsperson, so I had the presence of mind to follow the Recommended Wilderness Moose-Encounter Procedure, which was to get in the car and indicate to my wife, via a system of coded horn-honks, that she was to pack up all our equipment and put it in the car trunk, and then get in the trunk herself, so that I would not have to open the actual door until we had relocated to a safer area, such as Ohio.

This chilling story is yet another reminder of the importance of:

Selecting the Proper Campsite

Selecting the proper campsite can mean the difference between survival and death in the wilderness, so you, the woodsperson, must always scrutinize the terrain carefully to make sure that it can provide you with the basic necessities, the main one being a metal thing that sticks out of the ground where you hook up the air conditioner on your recreational vehicle. I'm assuming here that you have a recreational vehicle, which has been the preferred mode of camping in America ever since the early pioneers traveled westward in primitive, oxen-drawn Winnebagos.

Of course there are some thoughtful, environmentally sensitive ecology nuts who prefer to camp in tents, which are fine except for four things:

1. All tent-erection instructions are written by the Internal Revenue Service ("Insert ferrule post into whippet grommet, or 23 percent of your gross deductible adjustables, whichever is more difficult").

2. It always rains on tents. Rainstorms will travel thousands of miles against the prevailing winds for the opportunity to rain on a tent, which is bad because:

3. Tents contain mildews, which are tiny one-celled animals that are activated by moisture and immediately start

committing one-celled acts of flatulence, so that before long it smells like you're sleeping in a giant unwashed gym sock.

4. Tents are highly attractive to bears. When bears are young, their parents give them, as a treat, little camper-shaped candies in little tent wrappers.

So I'm recommending a major recreational vehicle, the kind that has a VCR-equipped recreation room and consumes the annual energy output of Syria merely to operate the windshield wipers. Other wilderness survival equipment that you should always take along includes:

- a hatchet, in case you need to fix the VCR;

- Cheez-Its; and

- a flashlight last used in 1973, with what appears to be penicillin mold growing on the batteries.

And speaking of penicillin, you need to know:

What to Do in a Medical Emergency

Experts agree that the most important rule in a wilderness medical emergency is: Keep your head down on the follow-through. No! My mistake! That's the most important rule in golf. The most important rule in a wilderness medical emergency is: Don't panic. To prevent the victim from going into shock, you must reassure him, as calmly as possible, that everything's going to be fine:

> VICTIM (clearly frightened): *Am I going to be okay?*
> YOU (in a soothing voice): *Of course you are! I'm sure we'll find your legs around here someplace!*
> Victim (relieved): *Whew! You got any Cheez-Its?*

Once the victim has been calmed, you need to obtain pertinent information by asking the following Standard Medical Questions:

1. Does he have medical insurance?

2. Does his spouse have medical insurance?

3. Was he referred to this wilderness by another doctor?

4. How much does he weigh?

5. Does that figure include legs?

Write this information down on a medical chart, then give the victim a 1986 copy of *Fortune* magazine to read while you decide on the correct course of treatment. This will depend on the exact nature of the injury. For example, if it's mushroom poisoning or a broken limb, you'll need to apply a tourniquet. Whereas if it's a snake bite, then you need to determine whether the snake was poisonous, which will be indicated by tiny markings on the snake's stomach as follows:

WARNING! POISON SNAKE!
ACHTUNG! SCHLANGE SCHNAPPENKILLEN!

In this case, you need to apply a tourniquet to the snake.

Fun Family Wilderness Activities

There are so many fun things for a family to do together in the wilderness that I hardly know where to start. One proven barrel of wilderness laughs is to try to identify specific kinds of trees by looking at the bark, leaves, federal identification plaques, etc. This activity is bound to provide many seconds of enjoyment for the youngsters. ("This one's an oak!" "No it's not!" "You suck!") Later on, you can play Survival Adventure, where the children, using only a compass and a map, must try to figure out what city Mom and Dad have driven to.

But the greatest camping fun comes at night, when everybody gathers 'round the campfire and sings campfire songs. Some of our "old family favorites" include:

I've Been Workin' on the Railroad

Oh, I've been workin' on the railroad,
With a banjo on my knee.
We will kill the old red rooster
We will kill the old red rooster
We will kill the old red rooster
And you better not get in our way.

Michael Row the Boat Ashore

Michael row the boat ashore, Alleluia!
Michael row the boat ashore, Alleluia!

Michael row the damn boat ashore,
    Alleluia!
Lenore threw up in the tackle box.

Camptown Races
Camptown ladies sing this song: Doo-dah,
    doo-dah
Camptown ladies been off their
    medication
And they are none too fond of the old red
    rooster, either.

After the singing, it's time for Dad to prepare the children for bedtime by telling them a traditional campfire story. To qualify as traditional, the story has to adhere to the following guidelines, established by the National Park Service:

1. It has to begin Many Years Ago when some people camped Right in This Very Forest on a night Exactly Like Tonight.

2. People warned them not to camp here, but they paid no attention.

3. People said, "I wouldn't go back in there if I were you! That's the lair of the [select one]:
   a. Snake Man!"
   b. Swamp Devil!"
   c. Giant Radioactive Meat-Eating Box Turtle of Death!"

4. But the campers just laughed.

5. "Ha ha!" were their exact words.

6. Until they found little Jennifer's gallbladder on the hibachi.

And so on. Dad should tell this story in a soft, almost hypnotic voice, lulling the children into a trance-like state in which they are aware of nothing except the story and the terror and the still, sinister darkness all around them and OHMIGOD HERE IT COMES . . .

And then it's time for everybody to "call it a night" and climb, all five of you, into the sleeping bag with Mom.

"Bad Advice" in
The Fish's Eye: Essays about Angling and the Outdoors

IAN FRAZIER

Some years ago, on a camping trip in the pine woods of northern Michigan, my friend Don brought along a copy of an outdoor cookbook that appeared on the bestseller lists at the time. This book contained many ingenious and easy-sounding recipes; one that Don especially wanted to try was called Breakfast in a Paper Bag. According to this recipe, you could take a small paper lunch sack, put strips of bacon in the bottom, break an egg into the sack on top of the bacon, fold down the top of the sack, push a stick through the fold, hold the sack over hot coals, and cook the bacon and egg in the sack in about ten minutes.

I watched as Don followed the directions exactly. Both he and I remarked that we would naturally have thought the sack would burn; the recipe, however, declared, "Grease will coat the bottom of the bag as it cooks." Somehow we both took this to mean that the grease, counterintuitively, actually made the bag less likely to burn. Marveling at the "who would have guessed" magic of it, we picked a good spot in the hot coals of our campfire, and Don held the sack above them. We watched. In a second and a half, the bag burst into leaping flames. Don was yelling for help, waving the bag around trying to extinguish it, scattering egg yolk and smoldering strips of bacon and flaming paper into the combustible pines while people at adjoining campfires stared in horror and wondered what they should do.

The wild figures that the burning breakfast described in midair as Don waved the stick, the look of outraged, imbecile shock reflected on our faces—those are images that stay with me. I replay the incident often in my mind. It is like a parable. Because a book told us to, we attempted to use greased paper as a frying pan on an open fire. For all I know, the trick is possible if you do it just so; we never repeated the experiment. But to me the incident illustrates a larger truth about our species when it ventures out-of-doors. We go forth in abundant ignorance, near-blind with fantasy, witlessly trusting words on a page or a tip a guy we'd never met before gave us at a sporting-goods counter in a giant discount store. About half the time, the faith that leads us into the outdoors is based on advice that is half-baked, made up, hypothetical, uninformed, spurious, or deliberately, heedlessly bad.

Greenland, for example, did not turn out to be very green, Viking hype to the contrary. Despite what a Pawnee or Wichita Indian told the Spanish explorer Francisco Vasquez de Coronado, there were no cities of gold in western Kansas, no canoes with oarlocks made of gold, no tree branches hung with little gold bells that soothed the king (also nonexistent) during his afternoon nap; a summer's march on the Great Plains in piping-hot armor presumably bore these truths upon the would-be conquistador in an unforgettable way. Lewis and Clark found no elephants on their journey, though President Jefferson, believing reports from the frontier, had said they should be on the lookout for them. And then there was Lansford W. Hastings, the adventurer and promoter of Sacramento, purveyor of some of the worst advice of all time. He told the prospective wagon-train emigrants to California that he had discovered a short-cut (modestly named the Hastings Cutoff) that reduced travel time by many days. Yes, it did cross a few extra deserts and some unusually high mountain ranges; the unfortunate Donner Party read Hastings's book, followed his route, and famously came to its grisly end below the narrow Sierra pass that now bears its name. According to local legend, the air in the Utah foothills is still blue from the curses that emigrants heaped on Lansford W. Hastings along the way.

People will tell you just any damn thing. I have found this to be especially so in establishments called Pappy's, Cappy's, Pop's, or Dad's. The wizened, senior quality of the names seems to give the people who work in such places a license to browbeat customers and pass on whatever opinionated misinformation they please. When I go through the door of a Pappy's or Cappy's—usually it's a fishing-tackle shop, a general store, or a bar—usually there's a fat older guy sitting behind the counter with his T-shirt up over his stomach and his navel peeking out. That will be Pappy, or Cappy. Sometimes it's both. Pappy looks at me without looking at me and remarks to Cappy that the gear I've got on is too light for the country at this time of year, and Cappy agrees, crustily; then I ask a touristy, greenhorn question, and we're off. Cappy, backed by Pappy, says the rig I'm driving won't make it up that Forest Service road, and I'm headed in the wrong direction anyhow, and the best place to camp isn't where I'm going but far in the other direction, up top of Corkscrew Butte, which is closed now, as is well known.

What's worse is that I crumble in this situation, every time. I have taken more wrong advice, have bought more unnecessary maps, trout flies, water filtration devices, and assorted paraphernalia from Pappys and Cappys with their navels showing than I like to think about. Some essential element left out of my psychic immune system causes me always to defer to these guys and believe what they say. And while the Lansford W. Hastings type of bad advice tells people they can do things they really can't, the Cappy-Pappy type of advice is generally the opposite. Cappy and Pappy have been sitting around their failing store for so long that they are now convinced you're a fool for trying to do anything at all.

Complicating matters still further is Happy. She used to be married to Cappy but is now married to Pappy, or vice versa. Happy has missing teeth and a freestyle hairdo, and she hangs out in the back of the store listening in and irritatedly yelling statements that contradict most of what Pappy and Cappy say. The effect is to send you out the door as confused as it is possible to be. What's different about Happy, however, is that eventually she will tell you the truth. When you return your rented bicycle or rowboat in the evening, Pappy and Cappy are packed away in glycolene somewhere and Happy is waiting for you in the twilight, swatting mosquitoes and snapping the elastic band of her trousers against her side. You have found no berries, seen no birds, caught no fish; and Happy will tell you that the birds were right in front of the house all afternoon, the best berry bushes are behind the snow-machine shed, and she herself just caught fifty fish right off the dock. She will even show you her full stringer, cackling, "You gotta know the right place to go!"

Of course, people usually keep their best advice to themselves. They'd be crazy not to, what with all the crowds tramping around outdoors nowadays. I can understand such caution, in principle; but I consider it stingy and mean when it is applied to me. There's a certain facial expression people often have when they are withholding the one key piece of information I really need. They smile broadly with lips shut tight as a Mason jar, and a cheery blankness fills their eyes. This expression irks me to no end. Misleading blather I can put up with, and even enjoy if it's preposterous enough; but smug, determined silence is a posted sign, a locked gate, an unlisted phone. Also, I think it's the real message behind today's deluge of information-age outdoor advice, most of which seems to be about crampons, rebreathers, and synthetic sleeping bag fill. What you wanted to know does not appear. Especially in the more desirable destinations outdoors, withheld advice is the most common kind.

I craved good advice one summer when I fished a little-known Midwestern river full of brown trout. Every few days I went to the local fly-fishing store and asked the guys who worked there where in the river the really big fish I had heard about might be. The guys were friendly, and more than willing to sell me stuff, but when I asked that question I met the Mason-jar expression I've described. I tried being winsome; I portrayed myself as fishless and pitiable, told jokes, drank coffee, hung around. On the subject of vital interest, nobody offered word one.

I halfway gave up and began driving the back roads aimlessly. Then, just at sunset one evening, I suddenly came upon a dozen or more cars and pickups parked in the high grass along a road I'd never been on before. I pulled over, got out, and crashed through the brush to investigate. There, in a marshy lowland, was a section of river I had never tried, with insects popping on its surface and monster brown trout slurping them down and fly rods swishing like scythes in the summer air. Among the intent anglers along the bank I recognized the fishing-store owner's son, one of the Mason-jar-smiling regulars. The experience taught me an important outdoor fact: Regardless of what the people who know tell you or don't tell you, an off-road gathering of parked cars doesn't lie.

In case you're wondering, this particular good fishing spot was on the Pigeon River near the town of Vanderbilt, Michigan, upstream from the dam. It's been years since I fished there, so I can't vouch for the up-to-dateness of my information. But unlike smarter outdoorsmen, I am happy to pass along whatever I can, because I myself am now gabby and free with advice to an embarrassing degree. I noticed the change as I got older; I hit my mid-forties, and from nowhere endless, windy sentences of questionable advice began coming out of me. An old-guy voice takes on its own momentum, and I seem unable to stop it even when I have no idea what I'm talking about. Sometimes when strangers ask me for directions on a hiking trail or just around town, I give detailed wrong answers off the top of my head rather than admit I don't know. When my hearers are out of sight, my reason returns and I realize what I've done. Then I make myself scarce, for fear that they will discover my ridiculousness and come back in a rage looking for me.

Outdoor magazines I read as a child featured authoritative fellows in plaid shirts and broad-brimmed hats who offered sensible tips about how to find water in the desert by cutting open cacti, how to make bread from cattail roots, or how to predict the weather by the thickness of the walls of muskrat dens. I wish I had down-to-earth wisdom like that to impart, but when I search my knowledge, all that comes to mind is advice that would cause me to run and hide after I gave it. The one piece of real advice that I do have is not outdoor advice, strictly speaking; I think, however, that its soundness makes up for that drawback. It is true virtually every time, in all lands and cultures. I offer it as the one completely trustworthy piece of advice I know, and it is this: Never marry a man whose nickname is "The Killer."

Other than that, you're on your own.

"Get Lost" in *The Grasshop*

PATRICK F. McMANUS

Several years ago I wrote what many experts consider the most authoritative work ever published on the topic of getting lost. The idea for the article germinated out of my observation that whereas millions of words have been written on how to survive when lost, absolutely nothing I had ever read dealt with the basic problem—how to get lost in the first place. What's the point of knowing how to survive if you don't know how to get lost?

Getting lost was a subject I knew first-hand. During my formative years, or approximately to age forty-five, I had deliberately contrived to discover all the various ways of getting lost, not only in the easy places, such as forests, mountains, and swamps, but also in less obvious terrain—vacant lots, shopping malls, parking garages, passenger trains, and tall buildings.

I discovered early in life that I had a natural talent for getting lost, a talent that through practice and discipline I honed to a sharp edge. By my mid-twenties I could set out for the corner grocery two blocks away from my house and, with practically no effort at all, end up several hours later in a trackless wasteland without the vaguest notion of how I had gotten there or how to get back. It reached the point where my wife would not allow me to go down to the basement to clean the furnace without map, compass, matches, and a three-day supply of food and water. I eventually compiled all my research on the subject of getting lost into an article entitled "The Modified Stationary Panic," which stands to this day, in the opinion of many, as the consummate work on the subject.

Although many scholars are satisfied to rest on their laurels, I am not. Several years passed without my becoming seriously lost even once, and I realized that I might lose the knack altogether, if I did not get out and do some fresh research. Thus, when my friends Vern and Gisela Schulze invited me along on a November deer-hunting trip in the snowy mountains north of their Idaho home, I quickly accepted.

The hunting trip started off in typical fashion. Vern assumed command and laid out the plans for the hunt, which included the admonition to me not to stray out of his sight. Vern and I have hunted, fished, and backpacked together ever since childhood, and I like to think that I have enriched his outdoor life immeasurably in providing him with countless hours of searching for me. Vern loves a good search.

Several opportunities to get lost offered themselves during the morning, but every time I thought to take advantage of them, either Vern or Gisela would come bounding out of the brush and herd me back to the trail. Then, about noon, I managed to give them the slip. I found a fresh set of deer tracks and followed them around the edge of a mountain—one of the best methods I've ever found for getting lost, and I highly recommend it. Soon the wind came up and snow began to fall, obliterating my own tracks so I couldn't retrace my trail, a nice bonus indeed! I can't begin to describe my elation upon suddenly stopping, peering around at the unfamiliar terrain, and discovering that I could still tell due north from my left elbow, but only because one of them itched.

I immediately began to perform the Modified Stationary Panic, which consists of running madly in place, whooping and hollering as the mood dictates. The panic will thus conclude in the same spot it began, rather than, say, in the next state. The Modified Stationary Panic, one of my own inventions, eliminates chances for serious injury, as often occurs in the Flat-Out Ricochet Panic, and also does away with the need for your rescuers to comb a four-county area in their search for you.

No sooner had I completed the panic than Vern showed up. I did my best to conceal my disappointment.

"I thought you were lost," he said.

"No," I said. "I was right here."

"Good," he said. "Maybe you've finally outgrown the tendency. Anyway, I just spotted the fresh tracks of a big buck going up over the mountain, and I'm going to see if I can find him. You swing around the north edge of the mountain till you come to an old logging road. You can't miss it. When you hit the logging road, follow it back to the car and I'll meet you there."

"Right," I said.

Ha! Vern's mind was going bad. Here he had just presented me with the classic formula for getting lost, and he didn't even realize it. "The old logging road you can't miss" is one of the great myths of hunting lore.

As darkness closed in, accompanied by an icy, wind-driven rain, I found myself scaling a precipice in the presumed direction of the mythical logging road. My spirits had long since ceased to soar and were now roosting gloomily in my hungry interior. About halfway up the side of the cliff, I paused to study a loose rock in my hand and recognized it as one that was supposed to be holding me to the side of the mountain. My plummet into space was sufficiently long to allow me time for reflection, although on nothing of great philosophical significance. My primary thought, in fact, consisted of the rudimentary, "Boy, this is going to hurt!"

Sorting myself out from a tangle of fallen trees at the bottom of the cliff, I took roll call of my various extremities, and found them present, with the exception of the right leg. Rebellious by nature, the leg now appeared to be absent without leave. Well, I could not have been more gratified. Not only was it getting dark and raining ice water, but I was incapacitated at the bottom of a canyon where no one would ever expect me to be. Even so, sensing that searchers might by luck find me too easily, I struggled upright on my remaining leg, broke off a dead tree limb for a crutch, and hobbled for another mile or so away from the beaten track. "Just let them find me now," I muttered to myself, struggling to restrain a smirk. "This is lost. This is real honest-to-goodness lost. It may be years before anyone finds me."

Detecting the onset of hypothermia, I built a fire to keep warm. But that is to put it too simply, too casually. No fire ever enjoyed such devoted attention. Cornea transplants are slapdash by comparison. The proceedings opened with a short religious service. Then pieces of tinder were recruited individually, trained, and assigned particular duties. Over the tinder I placed larger pieces, some approaching the size of toothpicks. At last the delicate structure was ready for the match. And another match. And still another match! I melted the snow from the area with a few appropriate remarks, and tried again to light the fire. This time it took. A feeble, wispy little blaze ate a piece of tinder, gagged, and nearly died. I gave it mouth-to-mouth resuscitation. It struggled back to life, sampled one of the toothpicks, found the morsel to its liking, and ate another. The flame leaped into the kindling. Soon the robust blaze devoured even the wet branches I fed to it, first by the handful and then by the armful. A mere bonfire would not do, I wanted an inferno. A person lost in winter knows no excess when it comes to his fire.

Next to the inferno, I built a lean-to with dead branches pried from the frozen ground. I roofed the lean-to with cedar boughs, and spread more boughs on the ground for a bed. Well satisfied with my woodcraft and survival technique, I stepped back to admire the camp. "Heck, I could survive here until spring," I said to myself. "Then again, maybe only three hours."

Once the lost person has his inferno going and his lean-to built, the next order of business is to think up witty remarks and dry comments with which to greet his rescuers. It's unprofessional to greet rescuers with stunned silence or, worse yet, to blurt out something like, "Good gosh almighty, I thought you'd never find me!" One must be cool, casual. Lying on the bed of boughs, next to the inferno, roasting one side of me and freezing the other, I tried to come up with some appropriate witticisms. "Dr. Livingstone, I presume," was one I thought rather good. Wishing to call attention to my successful fire-building technique, I thought I might try, "Did you bring the buns and wieners?" It is amazing how many witticisms you can think up while lying lost in the mountains. Two are about the limit.

I drifted off into fitful sleep, awakening from time to time to throw another log on the fire and check the darkness for Sasquatches. Suddenly, sometime after midnight, a voice thundering from the heavens jolted me awake. "Kneel! Kneel!" the voice roared.

So it has come to this, I thought. I stumbled to my feet and, wearing my lean-to about my shoulders, peered up into the darkness. A light was bouncing down the side of the canyon! And the voice called from above, "Neil! Neil! Have you found him?"

Within moments, Vern, Gisela, Neil, and the other members of the Boundary County Search and Rescue Team were gathered around me. It was a moving and dramatic scene, if I do say so myself. Calmly shucking off my lean-to, I tried to recall one of the witticisms I had thought up for the occasion. But the only one that came to mind was, "Good gosh almighty, I thought you'd never find me!" All things considered, that wasn't too bad.

From "Anatomy of a Crap" in
How to Shit in the Woods

KATHLEEN MEYER

High on a dusty escarpment jutting skyward from camp, a man named Henry, having scrambled up there and squeezed in behind what appeared to be the ideal bush for camouflage, began lowering himself precariously into a deep knee bend. Far below, just out of their bedrolls, three fellow river runners violated the profound quiet of canyon's first light by poking about the commissary, cracking eggs, snapping twigs, and sloshing out the coffeepot. Through the branches, our pretzel man on the hill observed the breakfast preparations while proceeding with his own morning mission. To the earth it finally fell, round and firm, this sturdy turd. With a bit more encouragement from gravity, it rolled slowly out from between Henry's big boots, threaded its way through the spindly trunks of the "ideal" bush, and then truly taking on a mind of its own, leaped into the air like a downhill skier out at the gate.

You can see the dust trail of a fast-moving pickup mushrooming off a dirt road long after you've lost sight of the truck. Henry watched, wide-eyed and helpless, as a similar if smaller cloud billowed up defiantly below him, and the actual item became obscured from view. Zigging and zagging, it caromed off rough spots in the terrain. Madly it bumped and tumbled and dropped, as though making its run through a giant pinball machine. Gaining momentum, gathering its own little avalanche, round and down it spun like a buried back tire spraying up sand. All too fast it raced down the steep slope—until it became locked into that deadly slow motion common to the fleeting seconds just preceding all imminent, unalterable disasters. With one last bounce, one final effort at heavenward orbit, this unruly goof ball (followed by an arcing tail of debris) landed in a terminal thud and a rain of pebbly clatter not six inches from the bare foot of the woman measuring out coffee.

With his dignity thus unraveled along sixty yards of descent, Henry in all likelihood might have come home from his first river trip firmly resolved to never again set foot past the end of the asphalt. Of course, left to his own devices and with any determination at all unless he was a total fumble-bum, Henry would have learned how to shit in the woods. Eventually. The refining of his skills by trial and error and the acquiring of grace, poise, and self-confidence—not to mention muscle development and balance—would probably have taken him about as long as it did me: years.

I don't think Henry would mind our taking a closer look at his calamity. Henry can teach us a lot, and not all by poor example. Indeed, he started out on the right track by getting far enough away from camp to ensure his privacy. Straight up just wasn't the best choice of direction. Next he chose a location with a view, although whether he took time to appreciate it is unknown. Usually I recommend a wide-reaching view, a landscape rolling away to distant mountain peaks and broad expanses of wild sky. But a close-in setting near a lichen-covered rock, a single wildflower, or even dried-up weeds and monotonous talus when quietly studied, can offer inspiration of a different brand.

The more time you spend in the wild, the easier it will be to reconnoiter an inspiring view. A friend of mine calls her morning exercise the Advanced Wilderness Appreciation Walk. As she strides along an irrigation canal practically devoid of vegetation, but overgrown with crumpled beer cans, has-been appliances, and rusted auto parts, she finds the morning's joy in the colors of the sunrise and the backlighting of a lone thistle.

Essential for the outdoor neophyte is a breathtaking view. These opportunities for glorious moments alone in the presence of grandeur should be soaked up. They are soul-replenishing and mind-expanding. The ideal occasion for communing with nature is while you're peacefully sitting still—yes, shitting in the woods. The rest of the day, unless you're trekking solo, can quickly become cluttered with social or organizational distractions.

But back to Henry, whose only major mistake was failing to dig a hole. It's something to think about: a small hole preventing the complete destruction of an ego. A proper hole is of great importance, not only in averting disasters such as Henry's, but in preventing the spread of disease and facilitating rapid decomposition.

More do's and don'ts for preserving mental and physical health while shitting in the woods will become apparent as we look in on Charles. He has his own notion about clothes and pooping in the wilderness: He takes them off. Needless to say, this man hikes well away from camp and any connecting trails to a place where he feels secure about completely removing his britches and relaxing for a spell. Finding an ant-free log, he digs his hole on the opposite side from the view, sits down, scoots to the back of the log, and floats into the rhapsody that pine tops find in the clouds. Remember this one. This is by far the dreamiest, most relaxing setup for shitting in the woods. A smooth, bread-loaf-shaped rock (or even your backpack in a pinch in vacant wasteland) can be used in the same manner—for hanging your buns over the back.

This seems like an appropriate spot to share a helpful technique imparted to me one day by another friend: "Shit first, dig later." In puzzlement, I turned to her, and as our eyes met she watched mine grow into harvest moons. But of course, "Shit first, dig later"—that way you could never miss the hole. It was the perfect solution! Perfect, that is, for anyone with bad aim. Me? Not me.

Unlike Charles, there's my longtime friend Elizabeth who prizes the usefulness of her clothes. While on a rattletrap bus trip through northern Mexico, the lumbering vehicle on which she rode came to a five-minute halt to compensate for the lack of a toilet on board. Like a colorful parachute descending from the desert skies, Lizzie's voluminous skirts billowed to the earth, and she squatted down inside her own private outhouse.

Occasionally it is impossible to obtain an optimal degree of privacy. Some years back, my colleague Henrietta Alice was hitchhiking on the autobahn in Germany, where the terrain was board-flat and barren. At last, unable to contain herself, she asked the driver to stop and she struck out across a field toward a knoll topped by a lone bush. There, hidden by the branches and feeling safe from the eyes of traffic, she squatted and swung up the back of her skirt, securing it as a cape over her head. But Henrietta's rejoicing ended abruptly. Out of nowhere came a column of Boy Guides (the rear guard?) marching past her bare derrière.

There are many theories on clothes and shitting, all individual and personal. In time you will develop your own. Edwin, our next case study, has a new theory about clothes after one memorable hunting trip; whether it be to take them off or keep them on, I haven't figured out.

For the better part of a nippy fall morning, Edwin had been slinking through whole mountain ranges of gnarly underbrush in pursuit of an elusive six-pointer. Relentlessly trudging along with no luck, he finally became discouraged, a cold drizzle adding to his gloom. Then a lovely meadow opened before him and its beauty caused him to pause. His attention averted from the deer, he now relaxed into a gaze of pleasure, and soon became aware of his physical discomforts: every weary muscle, every labored joint, every minuscule bramble scratch—and then another pressing matter.

Coming upon a log beneath a spreading tree, Edwin propped up his rifle, quickly slipped off his poncho, and slid the suspenders from his shoulders. Whistling now, he sat and shat. But when he turned to bid it farewell, not a thing was there. Oh, hell! In total disbelief, Edwin peered over the log once more, still finding nothing. The sky opened and it began to rain and a pleasant vision of camp beckoned. Preparing to leave, he yanked on his poncho and hefted his gun. To warm his ears, he pulled up his hood. There it was! On the top of his head, melting in the rain like a scoop of ice cream left in the sun.

Poor Edwin will not soon forget this day; he walked seven miles before coming across enough water to get cleaned up. Though I fear he was in no humor to be thinking much beyond himself, we can only hope he did not wash directly in the stream. To keep pollutants from entering the waterways, it's important to use a bucket to haul wash water well above the high-water line of spring runoff. But I digress . . .

Most of the foregoing stories are worst-case scenarios. I have recounted them not to scare you out of the woods, but to acknowledge the real perils and suggest how to work around them. Life itself is a risk; you could trip headlong over your own big toe or swallow your breakfast down the wrong pipe any day of the week. And have you ever tried to locate a toilet downtown—a task fraught with more frustration than any possible misfortune outdoors? Someone (not me) really needs to produce instructions for how to shit in the city.

I'll just say this: Disasters of elimination in the city can be more excruciatingly humiliating than those in the bush. Sometimes I think storekeepers, clerks, and tellers all must be terribly regular, "going" at home in the morning and then not needing a terlit (as my grandmother from Brooklyn would have said) for the rest of the day. If there is a stinking, grime-coated john tucked away in the far reaches of a musty storeroom, for some reason this information is as heavily guarded as the most clandestine revolutionary plans. In tramping around town, I've all too often encountered locked doors, scribbled OUT-OF-ORDER signs, EMPLOYEES ONLY plaques, or "I'm sorry, we don't have one" fibs. Sometimes, the only recourse is to streak for home and hope to get there in time. I'll take the backcountry, thanks.

So, get on out there. Find a place of privacy, a "place of easement" as the Elizabethans knew it. Find a panoramic view—one that can't be had with a Liberty quarter and the half turn of a stainless-steel handle. Go for it!

"Thieving Varmints and Tattered Gear," or "Annoying Animals I Have Known"

PHIL KNIGHT

There are a lot of annoying critters out there, both wild and domestic—packrats, mice, magpies, roosters, raccoons, possums, porcupines, poodles—but for sheer destructiveness, in my experience nothing beats a marmot. *Marmota flaviventris,* the yellow-bellied marmot, inhabits much of the Rocky Mountains, where I have spent most of my backcountry time over the last twenty-five years. Junkies of the worst kind, marmots possess an unquenchable hankering for salt in any form, and they will stop at nothing to get it.

Now, don't get me wrong; I am a big fan of wildlife of all kinds, and often prefer wild critters to humans. I have excreted a lot of blood, sweat, and tears defending native wildlife from greed and stupidity. But sometimes you have to draw the line. Thieving, scheming marmots, bent on satisfying their cravings, have repeatedly gnawed upon and damaged my gear, and once nearly robbed me of my footwear.

Years ago I backpacked in to the Spanish Lakes, in the Lee Metcalf Wilderness of Montana, a stunning location with jewel-like tarns set amidst alpine peaks and crags. Bolting a bit early from my landscaping job on Friday afternoon, I threw some gear in my car and blasted up to the trailhead, an hour from town. From there I made the nine-mile hike to the lakes in three hours, arriving in time to set up camp at dusk, tired and pleased with myself.

As I settled in at the lake, I heard the tell-tale piercing chirp of marmots on the rocky slopes near the lakes. Marmots inhabit dank holes among boulder piles in the higher elevations and spend much of their waking hours lounging in indolence on flat rocks, soaking up the sun, their fat carcasses draped over the rocks like slabs of butter melting on hot pavement. Lazier than sloths, they spend as much as eight months of the year hibernating. But something lacking in their diet causes them to seek salt with uncharacteristic zeal.

I tromped off in the morning and made a quick ascent of nearby Beehive Peak, a spectacular spire requiring a balancing act on a knife-edged ridge to reach the top. Upon my return to Spanish Lakes, I noticed something amiss with my camp. Someone, or something, had been in my tent! Pawing through the wreckage I realized that my sleeping pad was missing. Who would steal that grimy old thing? Then I noticed the chew marks on my pack. Some nasty beast had gnawed on a leather patch on my backpack. I deduced that a marmot had done the deed.

Casting about, I started searching for my pad, and finally found it fifty yards away, where a marmot had dragged it off and chewed on it, craving the salt that had soaked into it from years of night sweats and bad dreams. Gathering my ragged, chewed gear I hustled off to the valley, chastened and more aware of the dangers of varmints.

In Glacier National Park I went for a hike on the Garden Wall Trail, an unlikely path traversing vertical cliffs along the Continental Divide. I spotted a low-slung, furry beast hustling along the trail in my direction and halted, wondering what manner of critter this was. Bold is what I found out. It did not even hesitate, but ran straight up to me, stopped a foot away, and sat up on its bottom, its front paws held in the supplicating posture of beggars worldwide. It then darted forward, put its paws up on my gaiter-clad leg, and began licking my gaiter! Since my leg was protected I let it continue, fascinated to see its little tongue rasping at my garment. But it soon opened its jaws and made as if to gnaw on my leg with yellowed buck teeth, and I drew the line at that, pulling back, then kicking at the varmint to drive it away. It continued to follow me for over a hundred yards down the trail!

The Teton Range in Wyoming offers some of the finest alpine climbing on the planet. Mount Moran, an impressive peak in the range named for famed watercolor painter Thomas Moran, towers over six thousand feet straight up from the lake-studded floor of Jackson Hole, Wyoming. My goal was to ascend the precipitous Skillet Glacier to the summit.

After I dodged several belligerent moose on a harrowing bushwhack from Leigh Lake,

I scrambled halfway up Moran to the foot of the Skillet Glacier, where I made a bivouac camp by carving out a shelf on the glacier for my tent. That accomplished, I sat on a rock and took off my boots to air my sore, wet feet. I'd seen some low, dark varmints scuttling about, and heard the telltale shriek of a marmot whistle, but did not realize they had approached me till I saw one scuttling away, my boot clutched in its jaws! Visions of hobbling out on one boot flashed before my eyes as I jumped up and hollered, the marmot picking up speed with its prize. Desperate, I grabbed at rocks and began hurling them at the beast, and amazingly, I connected with the third throw. Grunting in pain, the varmint rolled over twice as my missile made its mark, dropping the boot and hustling away in a desperate waddle, its greasy tail describing frantic circles in the air as it ran. I hopped over in my stocking feet, ignoring the pain of sharp rocks, and seized my footwear before another marmot could get at it.

Rising at dawn, I donned my crampons and started up the glacier, leaving my tent in place. I made the summit of Moran by

8:00 a.m., then crept carefully back down the glacier, secured by my ice axe, only to find that marmots had again invaded my camp. Wise to their tricks, I had left my tent door open so they could go in without chewing through the side of the tent, as they had done on a previous trip to the Tetons. This time I had left a sweaty T-shirt hanging in the tent to dry, and discovered that the thieving varmints had eaten the neck out of it to get the salt!

In a city park in Spokane I was nearly mugged by marmots. Taking a break from scurrying about the city, I found a park bench near some shrubs and settled down with a sigh. As I did, a horde of bounding rodents appeared from the shrubbery and made a beeline for my location. Startled, I stood up, and as the dozen or so determined-looking marmots made for my legs, I jumped up on the park bench, afraid they would either bite me, climb on me, or both. The varmints gathered in a mob like an inner-city gang, peering up at me. Feeling a bit ridiculous, I made a mad leap over the marmot mob and scampered away, taking refuge in a bar.

Now don't go reigning vengeance on these animals, since they are only following their instincts and taking advantage of opportunities, like any of us. But do watch your gear, especially when the whistle of the marmot rings across the peaks, calling beasts to the feast.

"Fine Points of Expedition Behavior" in *The Cool of the Wild*

HOWARD TOMB

A good expedition team is like a finely tuned marriage. Members cook together, carry burdens together, face challenges together, and finally go to bed together. A bad expedition, on the other hand, is an awkward, ugly, embarrassing thing characterized by bickering, filth, frustration, and crunchy macaroni.

Nearly all bad expeditions have one thing in common: poor expedition behavior (EB). This is true even if team members follow the stated rules.[1] Unfortunately, too many rules of expedition behavior remain unspoken. Some leaders seem to assume that their team members have strong and generous characters like their own. But many would-be woodspeople need more rules spelled out. Here are ten of them.

---

1 Such as Don't Step on the Rope, Separate Kerosene and Food, No Soap in the River, No Raccoons in the Tent, Keep Your Ice Axe Out of My Eye, etc.

Rule No. 1: Get the Hell Out of Bed.
Suppose your tentmates get up early to fetch water and fire up the stove while you lie comatose in your sleeping bag. As they run an extensive equipment check, coil ropes, and fix your breakfast, they hear you begin to snore. Last night you were their buddy; now they're drawing up a list of things about you that make them want to spit. They will devise cruel punishments for you. You will deserve them.

Rule No. 2: Do Not Be Cheerful Before Breakfast.
Some people wake up as happy and perky as fluffy bunny rabbits. They put stress on those who wake up as mean as rabid wolverines. Exhortations such as "Rise and shine, Sugar!" and "Greet the dawn, Pumpkin!" have been known to provoke pungent expletives from wolverine types. These curses, in turn, may offend bunny rabbit types. Indeed, they are issued with the intent to offend. Thus the day begins with flying fur and hurt feelings. The best early-morning EB is simple: Be quiet.

Rule No. 3: Do Not Complain. About Anything. Ever.

Visibility is four inches, it's –10 F, and wind-driven hailstones are embedding themselves in your face like shotgun pellets. Must you mention it? Do you think your friends haven't noticed the weather? Make a suggestion. Tell a joke. Lead a prayer. Do not lodge a complaint. Yes, your pack weighs 87 pounds and your cheap backpack straps are actually cutting into your flesh. Were you promised a personal Sherpa? Did someone cheat you out of a mule team? If you can't carry your weight, get a motor home.

Rule No. 4: Learn to Cook at Least One Thing Well.

One expedition trick is so old it is no longer amusing: On the first cooking assignment the clever "chef" prepares a dish that resembles, say, Sock du Sweat en Sauce de Waste Toxique. The cook hopes to be permanently relieved of cooking duties. This is a childish approach to a problem that's been with us since people first started throwing lizards on the fire. Tricks are not in the team spirit. If you don't like to cook, offer to wash dishes and prepare the one thing you do know how to cook. Even if it's only tea.

Remember: Talented camp cooks sometimes get invited to join major Himalayan expeditions, all expenses paid.

Rule No. 5: Either Shampoo or Do Not Remove Your Hat for Any Reason.

After a week or so without shampoo and hot water, hair becomes a mass of angry clumps and wads. Looking like an escapee from a mental institution may shake your team's confidence in your judgment. If you can't shampoo, pull a cap down over your ears and leave it there, night and day, for the entire expedition.

Rule No. 6: Do Not Ask If Anybody's Seen Your Stuff.

One of the most damning things you can do is ask your teammates if they've seen the tent poles you thought you packed sixteen miles ago. Even in the event you get home alive, you will not be invited on the next trip. Experienced adventurers have systems for organizing their gear. They do not scatter it. Should you ever leave tent poles sixteen miles away, do not ask if anybody's seen them. Simply announce—with a good-natured chuckle—that you are about to set off in the dark on a thirty-two-mile hike to retrieve them.

Rule No. 7: Never Ask "Where Are We?" or "How Much Longer?"

If you want to know your location, look at a map. Try to figure it out yourself. If you're still confused, feel free to discuss the identities of landmarks around you and how they correspond to the cartography. Now, if you (a) suspect a mistake has been made and (b) have experience reading topographical maps and (c) are certain that your leader is a novice or on drugs, speak up. Otherwise, follow the group like a sheep.

Rule No. 8: Carry More Than Your Fair Share.

When the trip is over, would you rather be remembered fondly as a rock or scornfully as a wussy? Keep in mind that a few extra pounds won't make your pack more painful than it already is. In any group of flatlanders, somebody is bound to bicker about weight. When an argument begins, take the extra weight yourself. Shake your head and gaze with pity on the slothful one. This is the mature response to childish behavior. On the trail that day, steadily load the greenhorn's pack with gravel.

Rule No. 9: Do Not Get Sunburned.

Sunburn is not only painful and unattractive; it's also an obvious sign of inexperience. Most bozos wait too long before applying sunscreen. Once you're burned on an expedition, you may not have a chance to get out of the sun. The burn will get burned, skin will peel away, blisters will sprout on the already swollen lips . . . you get the idea.

Wear zinc oxide. You can see exactly where and how thickly it's applied and it gives you just about 100 percent protection. It does get on your sunglasses, all over your clothes, and in your mouth. But that's okay. Unlike sunshine, zinc oxide is nontoxic.

Rule No. 10: Do Not Get Killed.

Suppose you make the summit of K2 solo, chain-smoking Gitanes and carrying the complete works of Hemingway in hardcover. Macho, huh? Suppose that you then take a vertical detour into the jaws of a crevasse and never make it back to base camp. Would you still qualify as a hero? And what if you do? No one is going to run any fingers through your new chest hair.

The worst thing to have on your outdoor résumé is a list of the possible locations of your remains. Besides, your demise might distract your team members from enjoying the rest of their vacation. All expedition behavior flows from one principle: Think of your team first. You are merely a cog in that machine. If you're unable to be a good cog, your team will never have more than one member—and you will never achieve suavity.

From Chapters XXXII–XXXIII
in *Roughing It*

MARK TWAIN

Chapter XXXII

We seemed to be in a road, but that was no proof. We tested this by walking off in various directions—the regular snow-mounds and the regular avenues between them convinced each man that *he* had found the true road, and that the others had found only false ones. Plainly the situation was desperate. We were cold and stiff and the horses were tired. We decided to build a sage-brush fire and camp out till morning. This was wise, because if we were wandering from the right road and the snow-storm continued another day our case would be the next thing to hopeless if we kept on.

All agreed that a camp fire was what would come nearest to saving us now, and so we set about building it. We could find no matches, and so we tried to make shift with the pistols. Not a man in the party had ever tried to do such a thing before, but not a man in the party doubted that it *could* be done, and without any trouble—because every man in the party had read about it in books many a time and had naturally come to believe it, with trusting simplicity, just as he had long ago accepted and believed *that other* common book-fraud about Indians and lost hunters making a fire by rubbing two dry sticks together.

We huddled together on our knees in the deep snow, and the horses put their noses together and bowed their patient heads over us; and while the feathery flakes eddied down and turned us into a group of white statuary, we proceeded with the momentous experiment. We broke twigs from a sage bush and piled them on a little cleared place in the shelter of our bodies. In the course of ten or fifteen minutes all was ready, and then, while conversation ceased and our pulses beat low with anxious suspense, Ollendorff applied his revolver, pulled the trigger, and blew the pile clear out of the county! It was the flattest failure that ever was.

This was distressing, but it paled before a greater horror—the horses were gone! I had been appointed to hold the bridles, but in my absorbing anxiety over the pistol experiment I had unconsciously dropped them and the released animals had walked off in the storm. It was useless to try to follow them, for their footfalls could make no sound, and one could pass within two yards of the creatures and never see them. We gave them up without an effort at recovering them, and cursed the lying books that said horses would stay by their masters for protection and companionship in a distressful time like ours.

We were miserable enough, before; we felt still more forlorn, now. Patiently, but with blighted hope, we broke more sticks and piled them, and once more the Prussian shot them into annihilation. Plainly, to light a fire with a pistol was an art requiring practice and experience, and the middle of a desert at midnight in a snow-storm was not a good place or time for the acquiring of the accomplishment. We gave it up and tried the other. Each man took a couple of sticks and fell to chafing them together. At the end of half an hour we were thoroughly chilled, and so were the sticks. We bitterly execrated the Indians, the hunters, and the books that had betrayed us with the silly device, and wondered dismally what was next to be done. At this critical moment Mr. Ballou fished out four matches from the rubbish of an overlooked pocket. To have found four gold bars would have seemed poor and cheap good luck compared to this. One cannot think how good a match looks under such circumstances—or how lovable and precious, and sacredly beautiful to the eye. This time we gathered sticks with high hopes; and when Mr. Ballou prepared to light the first match, there was an amount of interest centred upon him that pages of writing could not describe. The match burned hopefully a moment, and then went out. It could not have carried more regret with it if it had been a human life. The next match simply flashed and died. The wind puffed the third one out just as it was on the imminent verge of success. We gathered together closer than ever, and developed a solicitude that was rapt and painful, as Mr. Ballou scratched our last hope on his leg. It lit, burned blue and sickly, and then budded into a robust flame. Shading it with his hands, the old gentleman bent gradually down and every heart went with him—everybody, too, for that matter—and blood and breath stood still. The flame touched the sticks at last, took gradual hold upon them—hesitated—took a stronger hold—hesitated again—held its breath five heart-breaking seconds, then gave a sort of human gasp and went out.

Nobody said a word for several minutes. It was a solemn sort of silence; even the wind put on a stealthy, sinister quiet, and made no more noise than the falling flakes of snow. Finally a sad-voiced conversation began, and it was soon apparent that in each of our hearts lay the conviction that this was our last night with the living. I had so hoped that I was the only one who felt so. When the others calmly acknowledged their conviction, it sounded like the summons itself. Ollendorff said:

"Brothers, let us die together. And let us go without one hard feeling towards each other. Let us forget and forgive bygones. I know that you have felt hard towards me for turning over the canoe, and for knowing too much and leading you round and round in the snow—but I meant well; forgive me. I acknowledge freely that I have had hard feelings against Mr. Ballou for abusing me and calling me a logarythm, which is a thing I do not know what, but no doubt a thing considered disgraceful and unbecoming in America, and it has scarcely been out of my mind and has hurt me a great deal—but let it go; I forgive Mr. Ballou with all my heart, and—"

Poor Ollendorff broke down and the tears came. He was not alone, for I was crying too, and so was Mr. Ballou. Ollendorff got his voice again and forgave me for things I had done and said. Then he got out his bottle of whisky and said that whether he lived or died he would never touch another drop. He said he had given up all hope of life, and although ill-prepared, was ready to submit humbly to his fate; that he wished he could be spared a little longer, not for any selfish reason, but to make a thorough reform in his character, and by devoting himself to helping the poor, nursing the sick, and pleading with the people to guard themselves against the evils of intemperance, make his life a beneficent example to the young, and lay it down at last with the precious reflection that it had not been lived in vain. He ended by saying that his reform should begin at this moment, even here in the presence of death, since no longer time was to be vouchsafed wherein to prosecute it to men's help and benefit—and with that he threw away the bottle of whisky.

Mr. Ballou made remarks of similar purport, and began the reform he could not live to continue, by throwing away the ancient pack of cards that had solaced our captivity during the flood and made it bearable. He said he never gambled but still was satisfied that the meddling with cards in any way was immoral and injurious, and no man could be wholly pure and blemishless without eschewing them. "And therefore," continued he, "in doing this act I already feel more in sympathy with that spiritual saturnalia necessary to entire and obsolete reform." These rolling syllables touched him as no intelligible eloquence could have done, and the old man sobbed with a mournfulness not unmingled with satisfaction.

My own remarks were of the same tenor as those of my comrades, and I know that the feelings that prompted them were heartfelt and sincere. We were all sincere, and all deeply moved and earnest, for we were in the presence of death and without hope. I threw away my pipe, and in doing it felt that at last I was free of a hated vice and one that had ridden me like a tyrant all my days. While I yet talked, the thought of the good I might have done in the world and the still greater good I might now do, with these new incentives and higher and better aims to guide me if I could only be spared a few years longer, overcame me and the tears came again. We put our arms about each other's necks and awaited the warning drowsiness that precedes death by freezing.

It came stealing over us presently, and then we bade each other a last farewell. A delicious dreaminess wrought its web about my yielding senses, while the snow-flakes wove a winding sheet about my conquered body. Oblivion came. The battle of life was done.

Chapter XXXIII

I do not know how long I was in a state of forgetfulness, but it seemed an age. A vague consciousness grew upon me by degrees, and then came a gathering anguish of pain in my limbs and through all my body. I shuddered. The thought flitted through my brain, "this is death—this is the hereafter."

Then came a white upheaval at my side, and a voice said, with bitterness:

"Will some gentleman be so good as to kick me behind?"

It was Ballou—at least it was a towzled snow image in a sitting posture, with Ballou's voice.

I rose up, and there in the gray dawn, not fifteen steps from us, were the frame buildings of a stage station, and under a shed stood our still saddled and bridled horses!

An arched snow-drift broke up, now, and Ollendorff emerged from it, and the three of us sat and stared at the houses without speaking a word. We really had nothing to say. We were like the profane man who could not "do the subject justice," the whole situation was so painfully ridiculous and humiliating that words were tame and we did not know where to commence anyhow.

The joy in our hearts at our deliverance was poisoned; well-nigh dissipated, indeed. We presently began to grow pettish by degrees, and sullen; and then, angry at each other, angry at ourselves, angry at everything in general, we moodily dusted the snow from our clothing and in unsociable single file plowed our way to the horses, unsaddled them, and sought shelter in the station.

I have scarcely exaggerated a detail of this curious and absurd adventure. It occurred almost exactly as I have stated it. We actually went into camp in a snow-drift in a desert, at midnight in a storm, forlorn and hopeless, within fifteen steps of a comfortable inn.

For two hours we sat apart in the station and ruminated in disgust. The mystery was gone, now, and it was plain enough why the horses had deserted us. Without a doubt they were under that shed a quarter of a minute after they had left us, and they must have overheard and enjoyed all our confessions and lamentations.

After breakfast we felt better, and the zest of life soon came back. The world looked bright again, and existence was as dear to us as ever. Presently an uneasiness came over me—grew upon me—assailed me without ceasing. Alas, my regeneration was not complete—I wanted to smoke! I resisted with all my strength, but the flesh was weak. I wandered away alone and wrestled with myself an hour. I recalled my promises of reform and preached to myself persuasively, upbraidingly, exhaustively. But it was all vain; I shortly found myself sneaking among the snow-drifts, hunting for my pipe. I discovered it after a considerable search, and crept away to hide myself and enjoy it. I remained behind the barn a good while, asking myself how I would feel if my braver, stronger, truer comrades should catch me in my degradation. At last I lit the pipe, and no human being can feel meaner and baser than I did then. I was ashamed of being in my own pitiful company. Still dreading discovery, I felt that perhaps the further side of the barn would be somewhat safer, and so I turned the corner. As I turned the one corner, smoking, Ollendorff turned the other with his bottle to his lips, and between us sat unconscious Ballou deep in a game of "solitaire" with the old greasy cards!

Absurdity could go no farther. We shook hands and agreed to say no more about "reform" and "examples to the rising generation."

"Let It Snow" in *Dress Your Family in Corduroy and Denim*

DAVID SEDARIS

In Binghamton, New York, winter meant snow, and though I was young when we left, I was able to recall great heaps of it, and use that memory as evidence that North Carolina was, at best, a third-rate institution. What little snow there was would usually melt an hour or two after hitting the ground, and there you'd be in your windbreaker and unconvincing mittens, forming a lumpy figure made mostly of mud. Snow Negroes, we called them.

The winter I was in the fifth grade we got lucky. Snow fell, and for the first time in years, it accumulated. School was canceled and two days later we got lucky again. There were eight inches on the ground, and rather than melting, it froze. On the fifth day of our vacation my mother had a little breakdown. Our presence had disrupted the secret life she led while we were at school, and when she could no longer take it she threw us out. It wasn't a gentle request, but something closer to an eviction. "Get the hell out of my house," she said.

We reminded her that it was our house, too, and she opened the front door and shoved us into the carport. "And stay out!" she shouted.

My sisters and I went down the hill and sledded with other children from the neighborhood. A few hours later we returned home, surprised to find that the door was still locked. "Oh, come on," we said. I rang the bell and when no one answered, we went to the window and saw our mother in the kitchen, watching television. Normally she waited until five o'clock to have a drink, but for the past few days she'd been making an exception. Drinking didn't count if you followed a glass of wine with a cup of coffee, and so she had both a goblet and a mug positioned before her on the countertop.

"Hey!" we yelled. "Open the door. It's us." We knocked on the pane, and without looking in our direction, she refilled her goblet and left the room.

"That bitch," my sister Lisa said. We pounded again and again, and when our mother failed to answer, went around the back and threw snowballs at her bedroom window. "You are going to be in so much trouble when Dad gets home!" we shouted, and in response my mother pulled the drapes. Dusk approached, and as it grew colder it occurred to us that we could possibly die. It happened, surely. Selfish mothers wanted the house to themselves, and their children were discovered years later, frozen like mastodons in blocks of ice.

My sister Gretchen suggested that we call our father, but none of us knew his number, and he probably wouldn't have done anything anyway. He'd gone to work specifically to escape our mother, and between the weather and her mood, it could be hours or even days before he returned home.

"One of us should get hit by a car," I said. "That would teach the both of them." I pictured Gretchen, her life hanging by a thread as my parents paced the halls of Rex Hospital, wishing they had been more attentive. It was really the perfect solution. With her out of the way, the rest of us would be more valuable and have a bit more room to spread out. "Gretchen, go lie in the street."

"Make Amy do it," she said.

Amy, in turn, pushed it off onto Tiffany, who was the youngest and had no concept of death. "It's like sleeping," we told her. "Only you get a canopy bed."

Poor Tiffany. She'd do just about anything in return for a little affection. All you had to do was call her Tiff and whatever you wanted was yours: her allowance money, her dinner, the contents of her Easter basket. Her eagerness to please was absolute and naked. When we asked her to lie in the middle of the street, her only question was "Where?"

We chose a quiet dip between two hills, a spot where drivers were almost required to skid out of control. She took her place, this six-year-old in a butter-colored coat, and we gathered on the curb to watch. The first car to happen by belonged to a neighbor, a fellow Yankee who had outfitted his tires with chains and stopped a few feet from our sister's body. "Is that a person?" he asked.

"Well, sort of," Lisa said. She explained that we'd been locked out of our house, and though the man appeared to accept it as a reasonable explanation, I'm pretty sure it was him who told on us. Another car passed and then we saw our mother, this puffy figure awkwardly negotiating the crest of the hill. She did not own a pair of pants, and her legs were buried to the calves in snow. We wanted to send her home, to kick her out of nature just as she had kicked us out of the house, but it was hard to stay angry at someone that pitiful-looking.

"Are you wearing your *loafers*?" Lisa asked, and in response our mother raised her bare foot. "I *was* wearing loafers," she said. "I mean, really, it was there a second ago."

This was how things went. One moment she was locking us out of our own house and the next we were rooting around in the snow, looking for her left shoe. "Oh, forget about it," she said. "It'll turn up in a few days." Gretchen fitted her cap over my mother's foot. Lisa secured it with her scarf, and, surrounding her tightly on all sides, we made our way back home.

"Foot" in
Planes, Trains, and Elephants

BRIAN THACKER

Innsbruck, Austria
June 1987

Everyone in the group had serious hiking gear on. They wore those tweed-like calf-length hiking pants (or are they shorts?), long woolen socks, expensive hi-tech walking boots, and micro-techno-fibro-thermo-wanko jackets. And all six of them had one of those fandangous telescopic walking sticks. I stood out just a little bit. I wore bright blue board-shorts with red cartoon dogs all over them and a pair of basketball runners. My walking stick was more of the old-fashioned kind. It was a rather bent and gnarled-looking branch.

Our guide, who must have been eighty, was already leaping up the steep mountain trail like a gazelle. I knew I shouldn't have had all those Jägermeisters the night before. And God, I felt silly wearing the feathered huntsman's hat someone in the bar had told me everyone would be wearing.

Our Austrian mountain guide's name was Hans (I would have been disappointed if it wasn't). A badge on his jacket had the word Führer embroidered across it in big red letters. Gee, and I thought he'd committed suicide in a bunker in Berlin, when all along he'd been working as a mountain guide in Austria. No, actually, Führer means "guide" in German. Mind you, the only guiding Hitler ever did was to guide his country to ruin and damnation.

Hans's English extended to one word: "Hello." He would use this for everything: "come this way," "look over here," "stop here," "be careful," and "hurry up, Brian, you're holding up the group."

I introduced myself to two fellow members of our hiking party, a couple in their fifties called Hal and Mary.

"Are you from Hawaii?" I asked Hal.

He looked at me in utter amazement. "Wow! You're clever. How did you know?"

Gee, it was hard. He was wearing a Hawaiian shirt and a baseball cap with Honolulu on it. There was also Clara, a sixty-year-old lady from Surrey in England. "This should be jolly good fun," she told me, with a basket of plums in her mouth. She looked as if she had borrowed her grandmother's hiking clothes from the 1850s.

Actually, I'm wrong. In the 1850s, women hikers didn't wear pants. They wore skirts (with flannel-lined tweed knickers to keep warm— mmm, sexy). The first woman to scale Mont Blanc (in 1838) did it in a skirt. She might have had an icy wind blowing up her fanny, but she travelled in style. She took an entourage of six guides (I suppose she took that many in case she lost one or two) and six porters. Six porters were *needed*, too, because the provisions they carried included two whole legs of mutton, six ox-tongues, twenty-four fowls, eighteen bottles of fine wine, one large cask of *vin ordinaire* (cheap plonk for the porters and guides), one bottle of brandy, three pounds of sugar, and a large supply of French glazed plums (one can never do any serious hiking without a good supply of French glazed plums, I say).

The Ecuadorian couple with us didn't have any French glazed plums, but they did have an enormous bag of "trail mix." It looked like something you'd feed to a cockatoo. They knew more English than Hans (but maybe less than a cockatoo). All of two words more. They knew "thank you" and "beautiful." They would answer every one of Hans's "hellos" with "thank you."

And finally, there was Jo—the reason I could join this Hiking Club trip. When I say *join*, I mean *sneak on*. I'd met Jo, an Australian girl who was working in Innsbruck, the night before. She said I could sneak onto the hike without anyone noticing (I couldn't have stood out more in my lairy shorts).

The first couple of kilometres were a doddle. Well, that was because we were in a cable car. We'd all met at the cable car station in the small town of Igls at 8:30 that morning. I have to say, I wasn't feeling too sprightly. Even though I'd only had four beers the night before, each beer came in a glass the size of a bucket.

"Hello, hello," our Führer encouraged, as we stepped out of the *Patscherkofel* cable car. The air was crystal clear and just cool enough to be positively exhilarating. With every mouthful of fresh mountain air, my hangover faded. We followed a steep trail straight up the lush green hillside covered in Alpenrose and other wildflowers. Mary seemed to know the names of all of them. The large city of Innsbruck below looked like a tiny hamlet from this height. It was like the view from an aeroplane.

Hans stopped to show us where we were going on his map. It looked like we were going a long, long way—and it also sounded as though every peak and every valley we were going to climb was called "hello." The hiking trails were marked in colours for degree of difficulty (blue = easy, red = intermediate, black = difficult). No one else seemed to flinch like I did as Hans kept pointing to blacks. I also noticed on the map that *hiking* in German was *bergwander*. Sounded like something you could buy at the Innsbruck McDonald's.

We trudged up a steep incline (I know it was steep because we were walking up what had been the downhill ski run during the 1964 and 1976 Winter Olympics). The ski-lifts looked out of place stuck in the middle of green fields. Particularly with fat, lazy-looking cows standing in the middle of the run.

I chatted to Hal and Mary. Well, when I say chatted, I mean gasped in between my puffing and panting. Hal and Mary were members of the Hawaiian Hiking Club (Hal was still amazed, by the way, that I knew they were from Hawaii). They had hiked in forty-two countries. This was their sixth hike around the Innsbruck area in eight days. Plastered all over Hal's backpack were badges from, among other places, Milford Sound in New Zealand, Patagonia in Argentina, the Lake District in England, and New York City (the only hiking there is hiking away from the muggers, I joked to Hal's blank response).

Still, they weren't a patch on Arthur Blessitt. He has walked 56,005 kilometres through 292 separate nations. He started walking in 1969 and is still walking. I have a feeling that he might be a few pumpkin seeds short of a trail mix. I say this because he's walked the entire 56,005 kilometres carrying a four-metre wooden cross (as in the Jesus variety). It is so big that it has trainer wheels on the bottom so he can drag it along.

He is doing this, he says, "because Jesus called me to give my life to carry the cross in every nation of the world." I'm glad I didn't get that phone call.

He hasn't had the cross the entire time, though. It was lost for a month by Alitalia Airlines. (He should have known better; Alitalia invented the term *lost luggage*.) It was also stolen, ironically, on the most holy day of the year and in one of the most holy places on Earth. It was Christmas Day in Assisi, Italy. He did get it back, only to almost lose it forever when someone set it on fire in Orlando, Florida.

Amazingly, and quite frighteningly, he's not the only one doing this. He has some competition. Keith Wheeler (whose motto is "Smile, because God loves you") has only visited a piddly 115 countries with his cross. I wonder what would happen if they bumped into each other. Would there be a fight? Would Keith be mighty pissed-off with the upstart Arthur? "Look, Blessitt, you may have travelled to more places than me, but at least I don't have wussy trainer wheels on my cross."

I was feeling like I'd walked 56,005 kilometres and we'd only been walking for two hours.

It wasn't because I was unfit, I might add, it was just that Jägermeisters and hiking don't really mix. Finally we came to a stop at a . . . bird house. Perched on top of this craggy peak was what looked like a bird house mounted on a wooden pole. Hans opened a little door and pulled out . . . a rubber stamp and stamp pad. Everyone in the group (besides me) plucked out a little green book from their packs. Hans gave me a quizzical "hello" when he saw I didn't have one. He reached into his pack and brought out a spare one for me. The book had *Fremdenverkehrsverband* written on the front. It probably simply meant "book." The Germans like using ridiculously long names to say something simple. Another example I found was the word for "rise" (as in pay rise). In Germany you would ask for a pay *gehaltsaufbesserung*. The *Fremdenverkehrsverband* was my *bergwanderpass,* or mountain hiking passport. All over the Austrian Alps are hundreds of these "bird houses" with little stamps and ink pads in them so you can put stamps in your *bergwanderpass*. My first stamp had the name of the peak (Boscheben) and the height (2,030 metres). I noticed Hal's book was full of stamps.

The bird box also had a guest book and a pen inside. Hal wrote "Another spectacular peak, another spectacular hike." Underneath that I wrote "If I don't make it back, can someone call my mum."

Hans was soon off again, leaping from boulder to boulder. We stopped often, but less to rest than to enjoy the view. I was bringing up the rear. Clara, who must have been in her sixties, was striding along next to me. "Gee, that's an impressive walking stick," I said.

"Yes. I only just bought it. It really is rather special."

"Oh, why's that?" I asked, rather stupidly.

"It has a vibration absorption system with anti-shock springs that can be turned on and off," Clara said proudly.

"You're joking!" (Well, I hoped she was.)

"No, and it also has this ergonomic cork handle," Clara said, handing it to me for inspection. I handed it back carefully. I was scared I'd drop it. It must have cost at least $200. I thought it looked too nice to take outside.

"I like *your* walking stick," Clara said, nodding at my beaten-up stick.

Yeah, right.

"Yeah, it's got a vibration absorption system, too!" I said, as I bent it down on the ground to form a bow.

The climb continued for another hour. Far below, the Innsbruck valley gave the impression of being poised above another world. Mountain peaks disappeared into a blue haze on the horizon.

Our second bird box was on the top of a windswept plateau. Patches of snow lay about in dirty clumps on the rocky ground. I wrote in the guest book, "You can all stick your telescopic walking sticks up your arse."

Not long after we left the bird box, we were traipsing through a field of snow. Then, within a space of thirty seconds, everything disappeared into a whirling white-out. It came out of nowhere. Only minutes before, we were bathed in sunshine. The air immediately became chillier. A micro-techno-fibro-thermo-wanko jacket would have been handy at this point. Through the gloom I could see Hans skipping through the snow. I could only see a few metres in front of me. Then suddenly the snow deepened as the track climbed steeply through sharp boulders.

Naturally, I stepped right into a snow drift. My legs were immediately sopping wet from the knees down, and my feet were soon squishing around in my runners, making it hard to grip the wet rocks. "Hello, hello," echoed Hans from somewhere in front. Somewhere far in front, that is. I scrambled on blindly for ten minutes.

Then, as suddenly as the white-out had come, it went. There was only one small thing that spoilt my relief at being in the sun again. I couldn't see the group. Oh, great. I didn't even know which way to walk. *I hope someone reads my message in the first guest book,* I thought. To be honest, I wasn't all that worried about being lost. I was more worried about missing lunch. I was just about to turn and walk the opposite way when I heard a faint "Hello, hello," from below. There, about fifty metres below, was the entire group standing together looking up at me.

"They don't like me very much, do they?" I said to Jo, when I finally clambered down to rejoin my hiking pals.

"Oh, yes they do," replied Jo, with a strained smile.

I was starving. "Where is *mittagessen*?" ("lunch" in German—it's always important to know meal times in a foreign language) I asked Hans. Hans pointed to a tiny dot in the valley below. That tiny dot was a mountain restaurant.

We dropped below the snowline into a sunlit valley. The trail ran alongside a small, clear stream and we crisscrossed it occasionally on narrow log bridges or stepping stones.

By the time we reached the restaurant I was so hungry I could have eaten my walking stick. Not long after that, I thought I might have to. I checked to see how much money I had in my wallet and all I found was twelve Austrian schillings in coins. That's about $1.20, and wouldn't even buy you a sniff of a goulash soup in Austria. I'd spent all my money on Jägermeisters in a drunken frenzy the night before.

Searching frantically through my wallet, I found an American five-dollar note tucked away behind my driver's licence. An American guy I'd been travelling with had given it to me as a souvenir. Sod the souvenir. When the waiter said he'd take American dollars, I couldn't hand it over fast enough. There was one small problem, though. Five dollars in an Austrian mountain restaurant, miles from civilization, doesn't buy much. I could only afford the *knackwurstsuppe*, which is a clear broth with a pork sausage floating in the middle of it.

Well, at least I had food. A few years later I went on a long hike above the Swiss town of Grindelwald, to the Faulhorn restaurant that can only be reached by a six-hour-return walk. I'd set off early and trekked up a steep, groomed walking track through the snow. With only an hour to go before I reached the restaurant, I stopped to take a photo and discovered I'd forgotten to bring my wallet. I'd been salivating at the thought of a long and ludicrously large lunch accompanied by a few icy cold beers, followed by a casual hike back to Grindelwald. Alas, there was no use continuing. I couldn't last the whole day without food, so I turned back. Yeah, I know we humans can survive days without food (an Australian fellow survived for something like sixty-three days eating only half a Mars bar and one of his socks), but I couldn't stand the thought of watching deliriously happy people devouring their giant schnitzels. I was hungry and mighty pissed-off, so I took what I thought was a shortcut through a forest. It wasn't short at all. I ended up clambering through thigh-deep snow repeating *Fuck!* over and over for the four hours it took me to get back down to the village.

There was going to be no hunger problem at the Café Pernblick. I took full advantage of the large basket of bread rolls, which eased my hunger but compounded my unpopularity with the rest of the group. Not surprisingly, we were the only people in the restaurant. It was in the middle of nowhere.

After lunch, we made a detour up another steep track and—half an hour later—reached another bird house. Following the stamping ritual, Hans stood on a rock and clapped his hands to get our attention. He then made a short and moving speech ("Hello, hello") before pulling a small clear plastic bag, with what looked like medals in it, from his jacket pocket. He motioned for me to step forward; then, to the rapturous applause of my fellow hikers, Hans pinned a bronze medal onto my T-shirt. I'd completed three peaks (which is very good for one day, Jo told me). And I not only received a bronze medal, but also a *Leistungs-abzeichenkasermandl* certificate (it probably meant "hike"). Clara proudly received her silver medal (for ten peaks), then there was a hushed silence while Hal and Mary stepped forward. Hal looked as proud as Hawaiian punch as Hans pinned a gold medal on his puffed-out chest for conquering twenty bird houses.

I wrote "Hello, hello" in the guest book.

The remainder of the walk was downhill. The low brush and low conifers gave way to a thick forest of pines. The path became a single-track road and we passed fields of freshly cut hay with its heady perfume. Farmhouses with traditional elaborately carved balconies and flower-filled boxes bordered the fields.

We reached the small village of Patsch just as I reached my I've-had-enough-of-hiking-for-one-day limit. Innsbruck still looked kilometres away. Just as I was seriously contemplating calling a taxi, Hans motioned for us to hop into a white van which was conveniently waiting for us on the opposite side of the road. We were back in Innsbruck by dusk, and after a long, long shower (I used all the hot water), I hobbled down to the hostel's restaurant for dinner. Sometime after seven o'clock I fell asleep, right into my goulash soup.

"Trout-Fishing" in *Love Conquers All*

ROBERT C. BENCHLEY

I never knew very much about trout-fishing anyway, and I certainly had no inkling that a trout-fisher had to be so deceitful until I read *Trout-Fishing in Brooks,* by G. Garrow-Green. The thing is appalling. Evidently the sport is nothing but a constant series of compromises with one's better nature, what with sneaking about pretending to be something that one is not, trying to fool the fish into thinking one thing when just the reverse is true, and in general behaving in an underhanded and tricky manner throughout the day.

The very first and evidently the most important exhortation in the book is, "Whatever you do, keep out of sight of the fish." Is that open and above-board? Is it honorable?

"Trout invariably lie in running water with their noses pointed against the current, and therefore whatever general chance of concealment there may be rests in fishing from behind them. The moral is that the brook-angler must both walk and fish upstream."

It seems as if a lot of trouble might be saved the fisherman, in case he really didn't want to walk upstream but had to get to some point downstream before six o'clock, to adopt some disguise which would deceive the fish into thinking that he had no intention of catching them anyway. A pair of blue glasses and a cane would give the effect of the wearer being blind and harmless, and could be thrown aside very quickly when the time came to show one's self in one's true colors to the fish. If there were two anglers they might talk in loud tones about their dislike for fish in any form, and then, when the trout were quite reassured and swimming close to the bank, they could suddenly be shot with a pistol.

But a little further on comes a suggestion for a much more elaborate bit of subterfuge.

The author says that in the early season trout are often engaged with larvae at the bottom and do not show on the surface. It is then a good plan, he says, to sink the flies well, moving in short jerks to imitate nymphs.

You can see that imitating a nymph will call for a lot of rehearsing, but I doubt very much if moving in short jerks is the way in which to go about it. I have never actually seen a nymph, though if I had I should not be likely to admit it, and I can think of no possible way in which I could give an adequate illusion of being one myself. Even the most stupid of trout could easily divine that I was masquerading, and then the question would immediately arise in its mind: "If he is not a nymph, then what is his object in going about like that, trying to imitate one? He is up to no good, I'll be bound."

And *crash!* Away would go the trout before I could put my clothes back on.

There is an interesting note on the care and feeding of worms on page 67. One hundred and fifty worms are placed in a tin and allowed to work their way down into packed moss.

"A little fresh milk poured in occasionally is sufficient food," writes Mr. Garrow-Green, in the style of Dr. Holt. "So disposed, the worms soon become bright, lively and tough."

It is easy to understand why one should want to have bright worms, so long as they don't know that they are bright and try to show off before company, but why deliberately set out to make them tough? Good manners they may not be expected to acquire, but a worm with a cultivated vulgarity sounds intolerable. Imagine 150 very tough worms all crowded together in one tin! *Canaille* is the only word to describe it.

I suppose that it is my ignorance of fishing parlance, which makes the following sentence a bit hazy:

"Much has been written about bringing a fish downstream to help drown it, as no doubt it does; still, this is often impracticable."

I can think of nothing more impracticable than trying to drown a fish under any conditions, upstream or down, but I suppose that Mr. Garrow-Green knows what he is talking about.

And in at least one of his passages I follow him perfectly. In speaking of the time of day for fly-fishing in the spring he says:

"*Carpe diem* is a good watchword when trout are in the humor." At least, I know a good pun when I see one.

"Bug Scream" in
Hold the Enlightenment

TIM CAHILL

The bug scream is a distinctive human sound. It is not characterized by volume, or intensity, or duration, but by the very sound itself: a kind of high-pitched, astonished loathing that combines the *eeewww* of disgust with the *waaah* of abject terror. *Eeewaah.* Every human has produced a bug scream at one time or another, and every human has heard someone else generate such a sound. Here is the First Rule of Vermin Shrieking: When a human being not oneself bug-screams, the sound is, by instinctual definition, funny. Cahill's Corollary to the First Rule is: Bug screams screamed by individual human beings *are not funny* to the individuals screaming.

Not that I consider myself squeamish. Quite the contrary. I've actually eaten bugs. More frequently, bugs have eaten me.

Not too long ago, for instance, I was walking across the Congo Basin in company with an American scientist, a filmmaker from *National Geographic*, three Bantu villagers, and sixteen pygmies. It was hot, and the forest contained what I imagined to be the better part of all the noxious bugs that have ever existed upon the face of the Earth, including bees and wasps, which I found particularly annoying, because all the creatures with stingers tended to congregate on me to the exclusion of my expeditionary colleagues.

Why me?

The scientist Michael Fay, of Wildlife Conservation International, said, in effect, "Because you're a big fat sweaty guy." He explained that all living organisms need salt, and that one of the factors limiting the abundance of life in the swampy forest was the lack of salt. The fact is, I was taller than Michael by several inches, over a foot taller than the biggest pygmy, and I outweighed everyone by fifty to one hundred pounds. Also I sweat a lot. I was, in effect, a walking salt dispenser, an ambulatory fountain of life.

There were at least half a dozen different kinds of bees in the forest, and every time I stood still for a minute or more, dozens of them took up residence on my drenched and sweaty T-shirt. Here, I thought, is an opportunity to observe nature in action. One interesting bee fact I learned is this: the little bastards generally only sting in response to dorsal pressure. If, for instance, you happen to be setting up your tent, and there are fifty or sixty bees sucking salt off your T-shirt, they will not sting unless you touch them on the back. For this reason, I found it necessary to walk with my arms held stiffly out from my sides, and to move slowly, in an angular and somewhat robotic fashion.

The problems occurred when salt-thirsty bees crawled up the sleeves of my shirt, toward the armpits, going right to the fountain of life, as it were. Then, no matter how robotically I moved my arms, there was some small dorsal pressure involved. It was worse when they crawled up the legs of my shorts.

Aside from the bees, there were tsetse flies, which can cause sleeping sickness, a disease characterized by fever, inflammation of the lymph nodes, and profound lethargy. Sleeping sickness is often fatal. And the insects that carry the disease are intensely annoying creatures.

They are long, thin, malnourished-looking flies, with skinny iridescent wings, and the ones I encountered moved so slowly I could actually bat them with a palm while they were in flight. Occasionally, I'd get a really good whack on one, and it would seem to falter in its aerodynamics, then wheel about in a lopsided loop, as if woozy and staggered. But it would stay on me. I could sometimes pop one I'd dazed three or four times using both hands—*whap, bap, whap, bap*—just like working out on a speed bag. The fly might back off, lose altitude, and then, as through an act of will, it would seem to straighten up and fly right, zeroing in on me again, and willing to take any amount of punishment simply to gets its filthy, disease-ridden, blood-sucking proboscis into my flesh. It was like fighting Rocky in the movies. Tsetse flies never quit.

Worse, you can't swat them on your skin, like mosquitoes. They have some kind of dorsal radar and, when threatened from above, simply fly away.

A pygmy who looked a little like a short, dark version of Jerry Lewis showed me the way to kill tsetse flies. Simple thing. Put a hand on your body some small distance from the fly and roll right over the son of a bitch from the side, like a steamroller. This process produces a nasty swatch of blood and bug guts. It is immensely satisfying.

Aside from the tsetse flies, we often encountered aggregations of fire ants, which are small and red and prone to swarming, gang stings. They frequently looked like pizza-sized hillocks of fungus on downed trees that lay across our path. Sometimes, walking along a nice, wide elephant path near such a tree, I'd see pygmies in the column ahead suddenly break into a strange hop-step sort of polka as they attempted to shake the fire ants off their bare feet and legs by stomping their feet. The convention was to yell *Formi* or "ants." In fact, watching someone out ahead do the Fire Ant Polka was all the warning anyone ever needed. It's awfully funny. When someone else is dancing it.

There were also driver ants, of the type with two-inch-long pincers. It is said that various native people in Africa use driver ants to stitch up wounds. It's supposed to work like this: The ant is held in the fingers and positioned with a pincer on either side of the wound. The ant then pinches, as ants will. Driver ants will not let go. At this point, one simply twists the nasty little body off the pincers. Instant sutures.

I don't know if people actually do this or it's just one of those oft-repeated travelers' tales. I do know that a driver ant bite hurts a lot, and that once they grab onto flesh, you can't shake them off, say, a sandaled foot, no matter how hard you stomp. I had to pick driver ants off my flesh, one by one.

Among the most unbearable of the insects was a kind of stingless bee, like a fruit fly, actually, called a melipon. Michael Fay said the word came from the Greek: *meli,* meaning honey, and *pon,* meaning, I think, incredibly annoying little sons of bitches. They arrived out of nowhere in clouds, so that, suddenly, every breath contained hundreds of melipons. They crawled into my ears and nostrils. Every time I blinked, there were several melipons ejected from my eyes, all rolled up and kicking their fragile little legs, like living tears rolling down my cheeks.

Sometimes, we crossed orderly columns of termites, thousands of them, marching along on some destructive mission or other. At night, they sometimes crawled in formation under my tent, and I could hear an unnerving clicking and clacking sound: termites, moving under my body in their thousands, all of them snapping their hideous little jaws.

None of these creatures ever caused me to produce a single distressed sound beyond *oww*. Halfway through my Congo walk, I believed myself almost immune to that universal human frailty, the bug scream. Vermin shrieking was something other people did, and they did it for my personal amusement.

I am, in fact, guilty of arranging certain situations designed to test and trigger the First Rule of Vermin Shrieking.

High school speech class, and here was my evil plan for the final assembly of my final year. There'd be four hundred students in the new auditorium, every seat filled, and I wanted to hear them scream.

We'd use the impressive new spotlights designed for stage plays. The best student actor I knew—and the only one I could trust to go along with me on this deal—was Dave Hanson, who would walk onstage wearing a funereal black suit. Stepping up to the podium under a single spot, Dave was to solemnly open a book, fix the audience with his best Vincent Price stare, and begin reading Edgar Allan Poe's merry little contemplation of corporeal decomposition entitled "The Conqueror Worm."

We knew what would happen. My fellow students, fearing Culture, would no doubt fidget for a bit. The poem postulates "an angel throng" sitting "in a theater." On the poetic stage, Poe has positioned "mimes," in the "form of God on high."

At this point, we'd begin to shrink the spot on Dave. The auditorium would become very dark as he dug down deep for his best shuddery bass voice on the verses we needed to really hammer home in order for the prank to work.

The mimes in the poem are—good Lord!— human beings. In their midst, Poe has "a crawling shape intrude." Bloodred, it writhes, it writhes. "The mimes become its food," and it—the bloodred crawling shape—is "in human gore imbued."

Dave could read that well, I knew. He'd pull the audience into the horrid realization of what this poem is all about. The last verse begins: "Out—out are the lights—out all!"

Which is when we'd kill the spot altogether, leaving the auditorium in total darkness, while Dave gravely intoned the last lines, which are all about the poetic angel audience sobbing heavenly tears because they realize:

That the play is the tragedy, "Man,"
And its hero is the Conqueror Worm.

Here, timing was important. We needed to hit them in the silence following Dave's recitation, but before the muttering and mumbling started. I had three confederates all set up for the nonverbal punch line. In the darkness, we'd run down the aisles of the silent auditorium, tossing out great handfuls of cooked spaghetti (still warm and a little damp). The spaghetti flingers all had a two-word line, a terror-filled scream, to be repeated as necessary: "THE WORMS . . . THE WORMS . . ."

Do it right and they'd scream. Most of my classmates would scream. Four hundred flat-out bug screams, or, more precisely, worm screams. Different creature, same sound.

One problem: Along with the rest of my worm tossers, I needed a pass to be in position at the back of the auditorium. A damn fine teacher named Fred Metzner demanded to know why the four of us wanted these special passes. He wouldn't accept "It's a surprise" as an explanation. Fred Metzner had learned not to trust student surprises.

And so, my plan was foiled at the last moment. Mr. Metzner described the idea as "juvenile," though I thought it was a good deal more mature than that. It was adolescent at the very least.

One night, several weeks into the Congo walk, I was just dropping off to sleep, lying in my tent, sometime around ten in the evening, when a half-pound centipede dropped from the fabric ceiling and onto my naked, sweating chest with an audible plop. Later, under my headlamp, I was to discover that it was not one of the poisonous ones. Just a normal Congo Basin jungle centipede and only about the size of an ordinary Polish sausage. It looked naked and pink, and was curled in on itself like something the dog left on the lawn. Under my light, the bug wasn't something you'd necessarily scream about.

But, half asleep, and in the dark, I had no idea what it was. Just something wet and heavy that seemed to have been dropped from a great height. I said *eeewaah*. I believe I said *eeewaah* several times in the darkness—a crescendo of half-awake terror—and when I brushed at my chest with blind, fluttering hands, I suddenly felt the heavy wormlike thing just above my wildly beating heart and swept it to the side. I said *eeewaah* several more times as I leapt to my feet, nearly stuck my head through the fabric of my tent, fell down somewhere near where "the unknown thing" had to be. Then rolled over, and finally came out of my tent like a scorched cat. All the time saying *eeewaah, eeewaah, eeewaah.*

The pygmies, all thirteen of them, were over in their camp, maybe fifty yards away. I could hear their battery-powered shortwave radio blasting out static-ridden music. The sound, as usual, was turned up into that range of irritating distortion in which it is impossible to tell reggae tunes from English madrigals. Pygmies, I had learned on my Congo walk, listen to the radio all night long. And they will always sacrifice fidelity to volume.

I had started out on this long jungle trek determined to get close to the pygmies, to understand their lives, their hopes, their dreams, their music. Most of all, I wanted to absorb a small measure of their knowledge of the forest. But they kept the radio on all night, never seemed to sleep, and I generally camped some distance away, just out of earshot.

So it was possible they hadn't heard me bug screaming.

But no, they were shouting and howling among themselves. And the howls were those of high-pitched and helpless laughter.

"What?" one of them called out to me in French, our only common language. I think it was Kabo, who was handsome as a homecoming king and one of the leaders. "What has happened?" he called.

I didn't know the French word for centipede. I don't know much French at all, but the word for insect isn't particularly difficult for an English speaker.

I *"insecte,"* I said.

Kabo strolled over, along with half a dozen other pygmies. I had scooped the centipede up onto a machete, using my notebook to avoid touching the thing, and was about to dump it, alive, a good distance from my tent. But the pygmies had to examine the creature that had caused me to say *eeewaah* several dozen times.

They aimed their one flashlight on the machete. The beam was very dim and yellow in color. The pygmies said some words to one another in Sangha, their native language, looked up at me, and, unnecessarily, I thought, began laughing again. They shook my hand and slapped me on the back and laughed until tears came to their eyes. It was, I thought, incredibly juvenile behavior.

Later that night, I could hear them in their camp, shouting over the static on the radio.

They used the word *mundele,* "white man," which has about the same connotation that the word *gringo* has in Latin countries. The noun is sometimes merely descriptive and void of nuance. Sometimes, like *gringo, mundele* can mean greenhorn, oaf, imbecile, or doofus. The meaning depends on the context. In this case there was silence for ten or fifteen seconds, then one of the pygmies would say *mundele,* meaning me, and the rest of them would begin howling with a kind of hilarity that I believed to be entirely inappropriate to something as human and unaffected as a few dozen simple bug screams.

It was in those moments of sweaty humiliation that Cahill's Corollary to the First Rule of Vermin Shrieking was born, screaming.

"Be Careful" in *Happy to Be Here*

GARRISON KEILLOR

The anxious weeks and days before the fall of the Skylab satellite certainly did focus new attention on the age-old problem of safety, as millions scanned the skies, dreading the descent of the enormous deadly object. Many tons of metal chunks, some with sharp edges, hurtling earthward, God knew where! Most of us must have been reminded that danger remains America's number-one safety problem, and perhaps a few were moved to check their own homes for hazards, for although some dangers can't be completely eliminated—such as a ton of lead heated red-hot by atmospheric friction dropping out of a clear blue sky and crushing your house to smithereens and leaving only a blackened hole in the ground for *Eyewitness News* to show where, moments before, you and your family had been pursuing leisure-time activities—there are dangers we *can* eliminate. These are things we have been warned against time and time again, and you would think people would learn, but do they? No.

For example, the number of persons who put their hands on hot objects annually would stagger you. "Don't touch it, it's hot," the waitress cautions as she places the steaming casserole on the table, and what do people do? They grab hold. Dumb? You bet, and yet you see people doing dumb things every day, and not just kids, either, but men and women with college degrees earning twenty-five to forty thousand dollars per year.

Item: A famous physicist whose research is so advanced that only two other persons in the world know the first thing about it walks straight out into traffic, thinking it is "smart" to thread his way among speeding cars and buses. They jam on their brakes, just in time, or heedlessly continue to race by, only inches away from his body!

Item: A famous surgeon, one of the very few who knows the human brain like the back of his hand and can go in there and cure unheard-of abnormalities and think nothing of it, places a skilled hand on the head of a strange dog—a tiny terrier, but even small dogs can leap high in the air if their instincts are aroused, and even a friendly pat can arouse them. "Why, he's never done that before," the owner says, trying to pull off the pet, whose jaws are clamped on Dr. Thompson's annular ligament.

Item: The editors of a famous newspaper, whose pages are read religiously by world decision-makers daily, lean across a conference table, debating an important editorial that might have far-reaching effects—*and waving sharp copy pencils to emphasize their ideas, as if they were toys!* They aren't. A pencil could poke somebody's eye out, like any other sharp stick.

Yes, many people don't have the sense that God gave geese. They just don't have both oars in the water. Millions of man-hours are spent worrying about the one chance in six hundred billion that immense man-made objects will fall from the sky and cream you; meanwhile, thousands of people wander off every year and get lost in deserted areas.

Stay with the group! You may think that if you get lost a major search will be mounted immediately by the National Guard, using the latest devices, including radar and infrared-sensing scanners, but don't count on it. For one thing, you may not be missed; your absence may not be noticed for days or weeks, and even then your friends will figure, "Oh, he'll turn up. He can take care of himself"—even as you wander, helpless and exposed, perhaps only a few yards from a road or a house. And even when the National Guard does come, it doesn't bring sensing devices. These are needed for national defense. If the Guard used its full arsenal of devices every time somebody got lost in this country, the Russians could walk right up Fifth Avenue without a shot being fired. No, the National Guard in this situation is just a bunch of guys beating the bushes, probably miles away from where you've wandered! But *don't wander! Stay put!* Of course, if you had stayed put, you wouldn't have gotten lost in the first place. So (assuming you will walk) don't walk straight, because you will wind up walking in circles. Bear to the right.

Don't eat wild plants, roots, berries, etc. People have been told a thousand times not to put strange things in their mouths, and yet as a result of the environmental movement, many assume that anything natural is good and won't hurt them. The best rule: Don't eat it. If you do, spit it out.

Eating itself, especially fish, is a danger area most people overlook completely, thinking, I won't choke, it can't happen to me. And yet every week we read about men and women just like ourselves dining in fancy restaurants and choking, which should be a lesson to the rest of us. Indeed, after a big choke scare you will sometimes see restaurant patrons cutting their food into smaller pieces, but they soon forget, and sometimes they go right on eating big forkfuls even as fruitless resuscitation efforts proceed a few feet away.

What is choking like? Those who have experienced it describe it as "the most humiliating thing that ever happened to me." There they are, paying good money for this food and having a wonderful time, talking and joking with close associates, when suddenly, still laughing, they feel the last bite go down the wrong way. Immediately, they sense the foolishness of the situation—to strangle on your own humor!—and they laugh harder and turn red and begin to die, surrounded by people who politely look away. Their obituary flashes before their eyes:

GUY CHOKES ON BEEF,
DIES ON FLOOR
Bystander attempts back-pounding procedure, but to no avail. "He was a good eater," say victim's friends, "and a great kidder."

The only hope is that Dr. Henry J. Heimlich, the discoverer of the famous life-saving anti-choking embrace, will be dining at the same restaurant and will come running over and perform the maneuver on the spot. And yet, to be hugged from behind by a complete stranger while you lie gagging on the floor: Is it worth it? How much better to be smart and not choke at all!

Remember, then: *Eat slowly, take small bites, and don't talk with food in your mouth.* How slowly? Very slowly, say experts. You don't have to dawdle or pick at your food, but do chew thoroughly. Don't "wash it down" with water. Chew it. Twenty times is a good rule for vegetables; for meat, thirty or forty is more like it. Fish bones are the real killers. You should shred the fish, remove all bones, and then follow each bite (small) with a bite of potato or bread, just in case. Better yet, avoid fish.

If, inadvertently, you should choke, don't panic. Stay where you are and motion for assistance. Don't jump up and run. This puts additional strain on the throat, which already has all it can handle.

Running itself is a danger area often pooh-poohed in the cause of "exercise" and "fitness," and yet the increase in running is leading to more and more cases of (1) tripping over things, (2) bumping into things, and (3) falling down.

Don't run. Walk. Facts show that walking for exercise is just as good as running and is much safer, particularly in the dark, on uneven ground, near busy streets, or in the house. Never run in the house, especially if you're tall. It's just plain dumb. And yet every year thousands of tall persons dash headlong into low doorways, decorative overhangs, and light fixtures.

Watch where you're going. Many feel it's a sign of shame to watch their feet while walking, and so keep their eyes straight ahead and "walk tall." They're looking for trouble.

Some falls can't be prevented. The victim is standing perfectly still and then suddenly— *ker blam!*—he's flat on his keister. Researchers say this may be due to a disturbance of the inner ear or to a simple lack of attention, but they don't really know for sure. Injury can be minimized, however, by keeping the feet well apart, the weight well balanced, and the arms slightly extended from the body. A few falls are caused by being cross-eyed, and nothing can be done about those, either. These people were warned about crossing their eyes for fun while in school, but they went ahead and did it anyway. Now they will just have to live with it.

A little common sense is our major weapon against danger. They say that if people would just *stop* and *think,* the chance of accidents would be slashed dramatically. Perhaps the specter of Skylab hanging over our heads might have knocked some sense into people—even though it fell harmlessly into the Atlantic and Indian oceans and parts of Australia—but probably not.

Chances are you will have read this article in very poor light. You knew it was wrong but you went right ahead and did it anyway. What can I tell you that hasn't been said a thousand times before?

ACKNOWLEDGMENTS

DAVE BARRY'S ONLY TRAVEL GUIDE YOU'LL EVER NEED by Dave Barry, copyright © 1989 by Dave Barry. Used by permission of Ballantine Books, a division of Random House, Inc.

"Bad Advice" from THE FISH'S EYE by Ian Frazier. Copyright © 2002 by Ian Frazier. Reprinted by permission of Farrar, Straus and Giroux, LLC.

"Get Lost" from the book *The Grasshopper Trap* by Patrick F. McManus. Copyright © 1985 by Patrick F. McManus. Reprinted by permission of Henry Holt and Company, LLC.

HOW TO SHIT IN THE WOODS: AN ENVIRONMENTALLY SOUND APPROACH TO A LOST ART, 3RD EDITION by Kathleen Meyer, copyright © 2011 by Kathleen Meyer. Used by permission of Ten Speech Press, an imprint of the Crown Publishing Group, a division of Random House, Inc.

"Thieving Varmints and Tattered Gear or, Annoying Animals I Have Known" by Phil Knight (the "Material").

DRESS YOUR FAMILY IN CORDUROY AND DENIM by David Sedaris. Copyright © 2004 by David Sedaris. By permission of Little, Brown and Company.

"Foot" (pages 29-37) from *Planes, Trains & Elephants* by Brian Thacker. Copyright © 2002 by Brian Thacker, published by Allen & Unwin (the "Material").

"Bug Scream", from HOLD THE ENLIGHTENMENT by Tim Cahill, copyright © 2002 by Tim Cahill. Used by permission of Villard Books, a division of Random House, Inc.

Reprinted with the permission of Scribner, a Division of Simon & Schuster, Inc., from HAPPY TO BE HERE by Garrison Keillor. Copyright © 1979 by Garrison Keillor. All rights reserved.

ABOUT THE EDITOR

Amy Kelley Hoitsma grew up in a family of five girls in Madison, Wisconsin, where summer days were spent at the neighborhood pool and family vacations were spent camping. Rather than a serene wilderness experience, they were a rowdy family affair, where telling stories around the campfire played an important role.

Today she lives in Bozeman, Montana, with her husband and cat, working primarily as a freelance graphic designer. She gets outside to ski, bike, hike, and camp at every opportunity.